CHILDREN'S ENCYCLOPEDIA
THE WORLD OF KNOWLEDGE

GENERAL SCIENCE

I0678674

Manasvi Vohra

V&S PUBLISHERS

Published by:

V&S PUBLISHERS

F-2/16, Ansari road, Daryaganj, New Delhi-110002
☎ 23240026, 23240027 • *Fax:* 011-23240028
Email: info@vspublishers.com • *Website:* www.vspublishers.com

Regional Office : Hyderabad
5-1-707/1, Brij Bhawan (Beside Central Bank of India Lane)
Bank Street, Koti, Hyderabad - 500 095
☎ 040-24737290
E-mail: vspublishershyd@gmail.com

Branch Office : Mumbai
Jaywant Industrial Estate, 1st Floor–108, Tardeo Road
Opposite Sobo Central Mall, Mumbai – 400 034
☎ 022-23510736
E-mail: vspublishersmum@gmail.com

Follow us on:

PUBLISHER'S NOTE

V&S Publishers is glad to announce the launch of a unique, set of 12 books under the head, *Children's Encyclopedia – The World of Knowledge.* The set of 12 books namely – *Physices, Chemistry, Space Science, General Sceince, Life Science, Human Body, Electronics & Communications, Scientists, Inventions & Discoveries, Transportation, The Earth, and GK (General Knowledge)* has been especially developed keeping in mind the students and children of all age groups, particularly from 6 to 14 years of age. Our main aim is to arouse the interest and solve the queries of the school children regarding the various and diverse topics of Science and help them master the subject thoroughly.

In the book, *General Science*

the author has broadly dealt with some interesting and fascinating Scientific facts like *The Atmosphere and its Composition, The Change of Seasons, Why do Plants and Animals become Extinct, The Vision of Owls, What is Milk made up of,* etc.

Each chapter is followed by a section called **Quick Facts** that contains a set of interesting and fascinating facts about the topics already discussed in the chapter. At the end of the book followed by a **Glossary** of difficult words and scientific terms is given to make the book complete and comprehensive.

Quick Facts

🐾 **When there are no more animals of a particular species left alive, that species is said to be extinct.**

Though our aim is to be flawless, but errors might have crept in inadvertently. So we request our esteemed readers to read the book thoroughly and offer valuable suggestions wherever necessary to improve and enhance the quality of the book. Hope it interests you all and serves its purpose well.

CONTENTS

SCIENCE

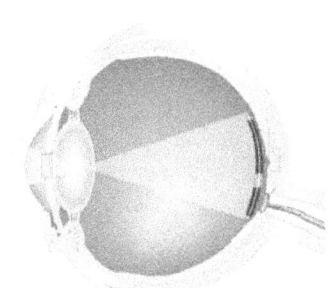

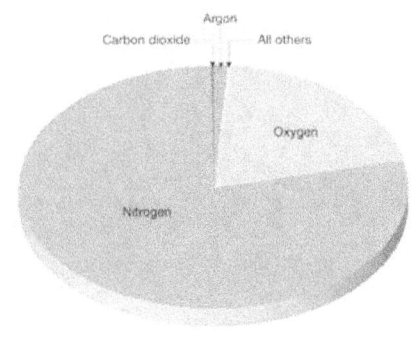

SCIENCE

Chapter - 1

THE ATMOSPHERE

The 'Atmosphere' refers to the blanket of air enveloping the Earth. It consists of gases, particles and various other materials. The main component of the atmosphere is nitrogen which occupies around 78%, followed by oxygen that constitutes 21%. The rest of the 1% is made up of carbon dioxide and other materials that include minute

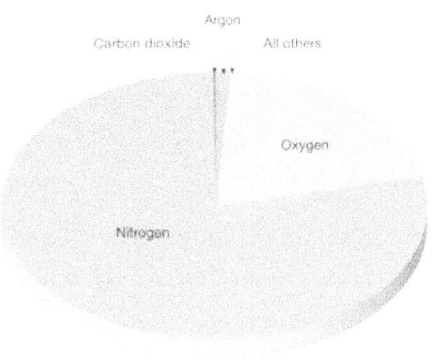

Gases in the Atmosphere

particles of water vapour, methane, carbon monoxide, hydrogen, nitrous oxide, ozone, neon, helium, krypton nd xenon gases. In addition to these gases, the atmosphere also consists of smoke, dust particles, volcanic ash, meteoric dust, pollen, etc.

The atmosphere is made up of many layers. The layers closer to the Earth's surface are denser than the one's away from it. The atmosphere extends up to 500 kilometers from the earth's surface and the pressure, temperature and density vary according to its height. The air pressure reduces to half as we ascend 6 kilometers from the Earth and similarly, the temperature falls by 1 degree Fahrenheit at the height of every 91 metres.

Based on its physical properties, the atmosphere has been divided into the following layers:

1. **Troposphere:** Accounting for 75% of the total weight of the atmosphere, the troposphere extends up to 17 kilometers from the Earth's surface. It is the most essential layer of the atmosphere as all living beings live in this layer. Moreover, rain, clouds, storm, etc. are all formed in this layer.

2. **Stratosphere:** Extending till 48 kilometers, the most important function of the stratosphere is that it absorbs the ozone rays radiated by the sun. These layers are extremely dangerous for human beings. There are neither strong winds nor varying temperatures in this layer.

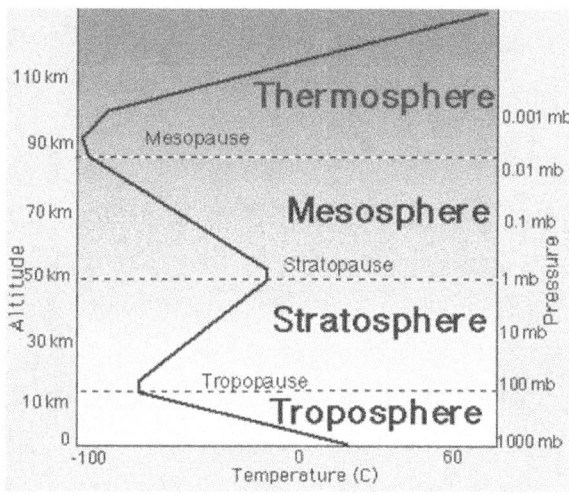

3. **Mesosphere:** This layer begins from a height of 50 kilometers from the Earth's surface. The temperature in this layer is very low and it is the lowest at a height of 85 kilometers.

4. **Ionosphere:** Starting above the Mesosphere, this layer extends up to 500 kilometers. It consists of charged particles that reflect radio waves towards the Earth and make radio communication possible.

5. **Exosphere:** This is the outermost layer of the atmosphere, and the density here is very low. Due to the presence of helium and hydrogen, the chief components of this layer, the temperature here is very high.

Actually, the atmosphere is extremely vital for our existence as it protects us from all the harmful radiations, meteors, etc. that come from the outer space.

- The thermosphere is made of the ionosphere and magnetosphere. The air density is the lowest and this layer comprises just 0,001% of the total volume of the atmospheric gases.

- In the ionosphere, sun radiations cause ionisation, i.e., the particles are electrically charged. The ionosphere reflects the radio waves employed in telecommunications.

- The magnetosphere is located above the ionosphere, at the external limit of the Earth's magnetic field. It behaves like a giant magnet, retaining high energy particles and thus protecting the Earth. This layer has the lowest density.

Chapter - 2

AN APPLE A DAY KEEPS THE DOCTOR AWAY

There is an age-old saying, "An apple a day, keeps the doctor away." But is it actually true? Does an apple actually have the properties to keep all diseases at bay? The answer is NO.

This saying was just made as a polite way of making people realise that eating apples is a good habit as it prevents *constipation* and other related ailments. The juice of a raw apple is believed to help in the *fermentation of undigested food*.

Though people of modern times find it arguable, it is unquestionable that apple is good for health. An apple has high nutritive value due to which eating it is suggested as a habit one should develop, particularly the children and youngsters. Even older people can be benefitted by eating this fruit daily.

Some people have modified the saying as, "An apple a day, keeps the dentist away." This is so because it is believed that biting an apple helps remove the food particles lodged between the teeth effectively. It is said that eating an apple between meals and brushing our teeth in the morning and before retiring for the night is the best way to maintain oral health.

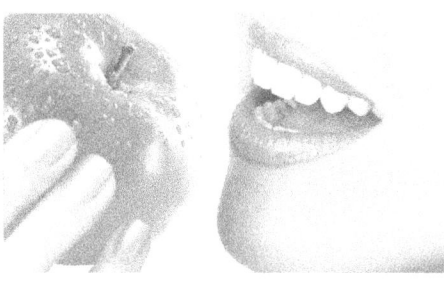

Due to its nutritional values, an apple is also believed to prevent diseases, such as *scurvy*, *night blindness*, etc. Since apples are rich in Vitamin A, C, cellulose and carbohydrates, they help in purifying blood, healing wounds, provide protection from cold, etc. They also assist in building strong bones, teeth and gums.

Eaten raw for taste and beneficial nutrients, an apple contains 80% water, while the remaining matter contains ascorbic acid (Vitamin C), sugar, other acids and rough indigestible matter.

Apart from being eaten raw, apples are also used to prepare sweet dishes, such as apple pie, etc. Cider is also brewed from fermented apples.

Apples are a member of the *Rosaceae* family. They are usually red, yellow, or green in colour in their ripened state. They grow in temperate zones, in relatively cold weather.

By the end of 300 A.D., 37 varieties of apples were named by a Roman writer. However, in today's date, various varieties of apples are available, which differ in sweetness and flavour.

- A fresh apple is an ideal, healthy snack for you because it's easy to carry, quite filling, juicy and refreshing. Some varieties provide you with a good source of Vitamin C, which is an antioxidant and helps to improve and maintain your immune system.

- Apples also carry relatively low calories and contain high level of fructose. This natural sugar, although sweeter than sucrose (main component of cane sugar), gets metabolised slowly in the body, thereby helping us to control our blood sugar levels.

- In herbal medicine, you'll see people using ripe, uncooked apples to treat constipation, while you can eat it stewed for treating diarrhoea and gastroenteritis. You can also use apples in poultices for skin inflammations.

Chapter - 3

WHY DO WE GET PINS AND NEEDLES?

The tingling sensation that we get in our hands, feet, arms, or legs after they haven't been moved for some time is because the blood begins to circulate again in those parts of our body. In scientific terms, this sensation is called *Paresthesia*; however, it is generally referred to as *pins and needles*.

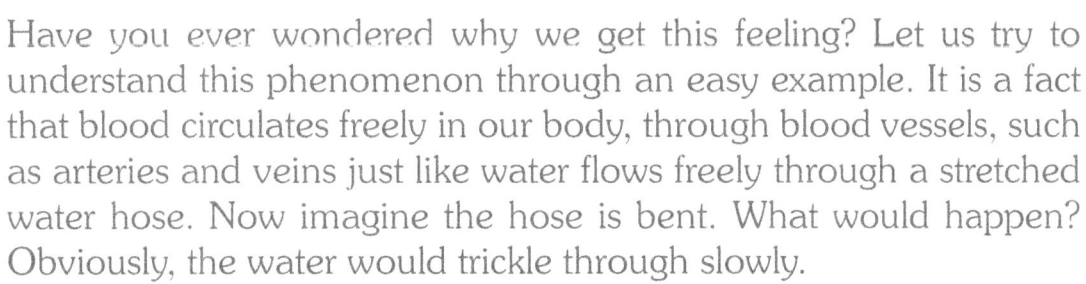

For example, after sitting for a long time with our legs crossed, we feel numbness when we try to stand up. We often refer to it as the legs 'falling asleep'. This happens due to the change when the blood begins to circulate in our legs again.

Have you ever wondered why we get this feeling? Let us try to understand this phenomenon through an easy example. It is a fact that blood circulates freely in our body, through blood vessels, such as arteries and veins just like water flows freely through a stretched water hose. Now imagine the hose is bent. What would happen? Obviously, the water would trickle through slowly.

Something similar happens in the case of the transportation of blood in our body. It has two main functions: (a) To supply food and oxygen to different parts of the body, and (b) To collect all the poisonous wastes. This flow is restricted if we block the path of our body parts for a long time. Due to this, the poisonous

Paresthesia in Hands

wastes get collected and this blocks the nerve cells from carrying any kind of messages from the affected body part to the brain. This leads to a feeling of numbness.

When the body part is stretched after that, there is a sudden rush of blood into the body part. Imagine this with the help of the water hose example again. After bending the water hose, if it is stretched again, it is obvious that water would be allowed to flow freely again, causing a sudden rush in the water hose.

Exercise to Prevent Paresthesia

Similarly, when the transportation system of our body is released of the blockage, the blood begins to circulate freely again. It is this resumption of blood circulation that causes the *tingling sensation or pins and needles.*

This situation can be of two types, *transient or chronic. Transient paresthesia* is basically the numbness that we experience commonly. It is caused because of excessive pressure being applied on a nerve which leads to stopping its function temporarily. However, *chronic paresthesia* indicates a problem with the functioning of the neurons, which may require special medical attention.

- Paresthesia sensations can be described in many different ways, including tingling, numbness, pins and needles, itching and burning. Paresthetic sensations may be accompanied by pain and other symptoms depending on the part of the body that is affected. Any associated symptoms can help your doctor make a diagnosis.

- Paresthesia usually arises from nerve compression (pressure or entrapment) or damage. Paresthesia can be a symptom of a wide variety of diseases, or disorders or due to injuries to the nerves.

- Temporary paresthesia can be due to any activity that causes prolonged pressure on a nerve or nerves, such as sitting cross legged or bicycling a long distance. Paresthesia can also occur with moderate to severe orthopedic conditions, as well as disorders and diseases that damage the nervous system.

- Because paresthesia can be due to a nervous system disease or nerve damage, failure to seek treatment can result in complications and permanent damage. The general symptoms are: Chronic pain, Inability to breathe on your own, Paralysis, Permanent loss of sensation, etc.

Chapter - 4

THE CHANGE OF SEASONS

The Earth rotates on its own axis and also revolves around the Sun. *Day and night are caused due to the Earth's rotation around its axis* that makes a vertical angle of 23.5 degrees. It is indeed because of this axis that as the Earth revolves around the Sun, its rays hit the Earth's surface at different angles and at different times of the year at one place.

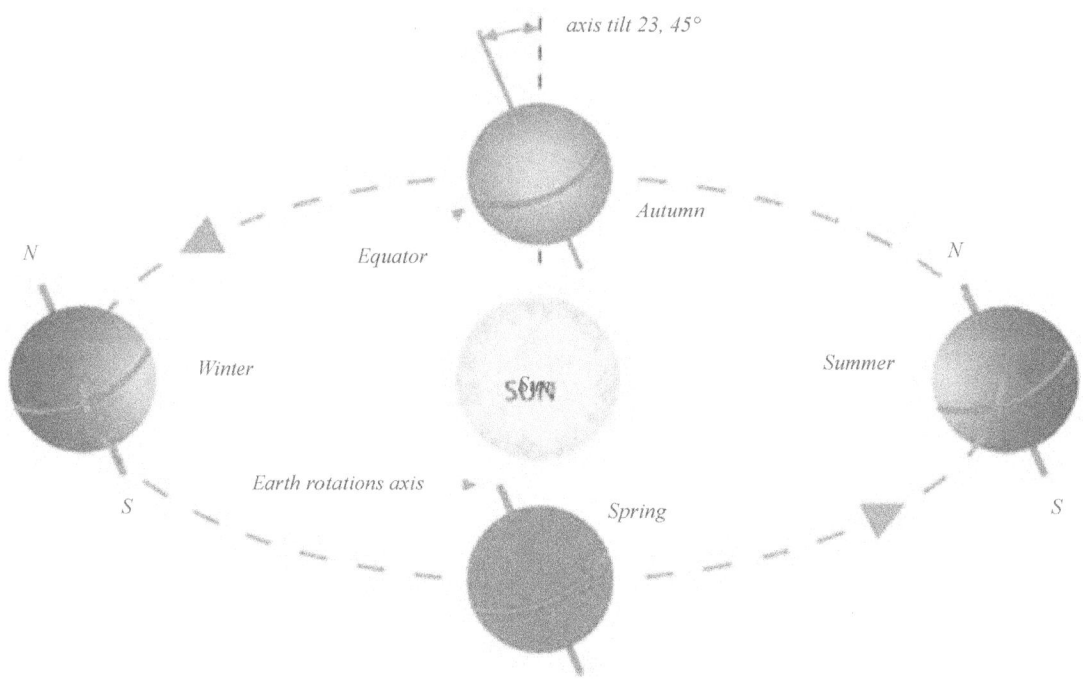

Formation of Different Seasons

Because of the variations in the angles, the solar heat gets distributed differently throughout the year at the same place. This uneven distribution of the solar heat causes the *change in seasons*.

Around June, the northern hemisphere is tilted towards the Sun and this causes summer in Europe, Asia and North America. Similarly, six months later, when the southern hemisphere is tilted towards the Sun, it experiences summer while the northern hemisphere experiences winter.

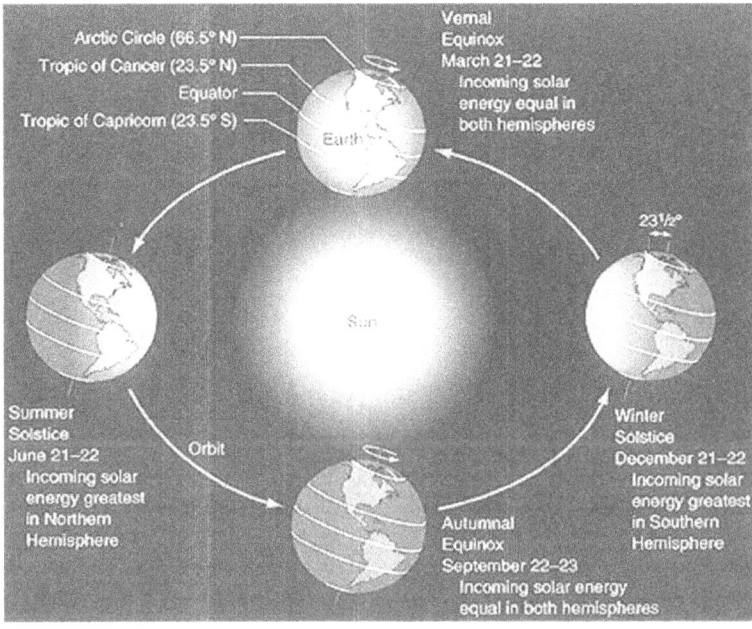

Summer Solstice, Winter Solstice and Equinoxes

March 21 and September 23 are two special dates as on these two days, the Sun is exactly over the Equator causing the duration of the day and night same (12 hours) at every place on the Earth. These dates are also called as **Equinoxes**. Between March 21 and June 21, the Sun advances towards the Tropic of Cancer, resulting in summer season in the northern hemisphere. This means longer days and shorter nights. It is during this time that the southern hemisphere experiences winters.

Between June 21 and December 22, the Sun moves towards the Tropic of

Globe showing the Tropic of Cancer

Capricorn, causing summers in the southern hemisphere and winters in the northern hemisphere. It is at this time that the northern hemisphere experiences shorter days and longer nights. After December 22, the Sun once again starts moving towards the north and reaches the equator on March 21. During this period, the days in the northern hemisphere once again start getting longer than the nights.

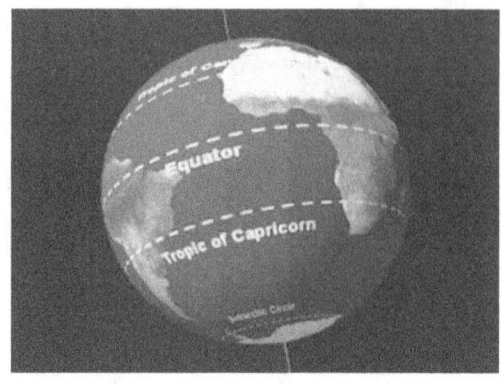

Globe Showing the Tropic of Capricorn

During the months of March and September, due to the Sun being overhead on the Equator, the hemispheres either experience *autumn or spring*.

It is thus the rotation of the Earth around its own inclined axis and its revolution around the Sun that causes the change in seasons from summer to winter in different hemispheres and also the transition from day to night.

Quick Facts

- The seasons result from the Earth's axis being tilted to its orbital plane. Basically, the Earth's axis deviates by an angle of approximately 23.5 degrees. Thus, at any given time during summer or winter, one part of the planet is more directly exposed to the rays of the Sun. This exposure alternates as the Earth revolves in its orbit. Therefore, at any given time, regardless of season, the northern and southern hemispheres experience opposite seasons. This is known as the Axial Tilt.

- The effect of axial tilt is observable as the change in day length and altitude of the Sun at noon (the culmination of the Sun) during a year.

- A season is a subdivision of the year, marked by changes in weather, ecology, and hours of daylight. Seasons result from the yearly revolution of the Earth around the Sun and the tilt of the Earth's axis relative to the plane of revolution.

- In temperate and polar regions, the seasons are marked by changes in the intensity of sunlight that reaches the Earth's surface, variations of which may cause animals to go into hibernation or to migrate, and plants to be dormant.

- During May, June and July, the northern hemisphere is exposed to more direct sunlight because the hemisphere faces the sun. The same is true of the southern hemisphere in November, December and January. It is the tilt of the Earth that causes the Sun to be higher in the sky during the summer months which increases the solar flux. However, due to seasonal lag, June, July and August are the hottest months in the northern hemisphere and December, January and February are the hottest months in the southern hemisphere.

Chapter - 5

WHY DO PLANTS AND ANIMALS BECOME EXTINCT?

At the time Charles Darwin proposed his theory of, 'Survival of the Fittest', it entered into many controversies and received a lot of criticism. However, in due course of time, it started receiving wider acceptance as it was found that certain species were found to be either extinct or were facing extinction due to reasons explained by Darwin in his theory.

Charles Darwin

Since the time of evolution of animals and plants, many species have become entirely extinct. On the other hand, certain species are facing the problem of becoming extinct. The conservation of these species has drawn alarming attention all over the world. Such species are called, the the 'endangered species'.

Deforestation

The causes that have led to certain species becoming endangered are both natural and man-made. One of the primary reasons for this predicament is the ever-increasing human population. In order to fulfill their needs, human beings encroach upon more and more forest land, leading to scarcity of land for wildlife to survive.

Migration of Birds

To fulfill human needs, heaths and forests have been destructed to make farming space, large-scale wood is deforested and more and more industries are being set up. Due to these reasons, among many others, wildlife suffers a lot.

Another reason for the extinction is *hunting* and *poaching*. Man has hunted various species to extinction, the examples of which are the auk and dodo. Pollution is another factor that leads to this unpleasant phenomenon. Every year millions of birds die painful deaths because of withering feathers as they get covered by sticky black oil from oil spills.

Some natural factors, such as unsuitable weather conditions, lack of food, natural calamities, etc. also contribute to the *extinction of plants and animals*.

Plants that need special measures of protection include helleborine, cheddar pink, monkey orchid, tufted saxifrage, alpine catchfly, and alpine

gentian. On the other hand, animals facing extinction are elephants, tigers, lions, ocelot, humpbacks, whale, panda, leopard, rhinoceros, puma, polar bear, the giant sable antelope, etc.

The preservation of these species has drawn attention both at national and international levels. Effective measures are being taken to preserve wildlife, such as, creation of *sanctuaries, implementation of stringent laws against poaching*, etc.

Quick Facts

- **Plants can become endangered as many of the same ways animals become endangered. Although conservation attempts can be made to save the endangered plant species, help often comes too late.**

- **Many factors can cause a plant to become endangered. Many of the same things that endanger animals, endanger plants too. The main cause of a plant species to become endangered is the loss of its natural habitat. A large reason this occurs is because of the expansion of mankind. As the human population grows, the more land mankind needs to comfortably survive. Unfortunately, as this improves the lives of humans, it threatens the survival of many plant species.**

- **Loss of natural plants habitats is also caused by an increase in wild fires. Over the years wild fires have began to intensify. Many believe this is caused by global warming. As the temperatures rise the more wild fires appear. This causes many plant species to loose their natural habitat.**

- Other forces of nature can also threaten plant species. For example: Severe droughts can cause large numbers of plant species to die and possibly become extinct.

- Loss of a plant habitat also occurs due to the agricultural industry. As the need for more agriculture increases, the need for more land also increases. Land is often cleared to make pastures or crops. This causes plants to loose their habitat. Grazing animals can threaten many plant species as well.

- Plants can also become endangered by the intent of mankind. Many rare plants are often collected by mankind for their rare beauty. These valuable plants can often be found in florist shops and nurseries.

- When there are no more animals of a particular species left alive, that species is said to be extinct.

Chapter - 6

THE VISION OF OWLS

An owl can rarely be seen during the day time. This is because while most birds are *diurnal* (active in the daytime), owls are *nocturnal* creatures (active at night) that 'come to life' in the night. The physical features of an owl include a large head, big *eyes*, sharp claws, short neck and broad wings.

An Owl

Around *130 species of owls* are known to us today. Some countries regard owls as auspicious creatures, while others consider them a symbol of *wealth and wisdom*.

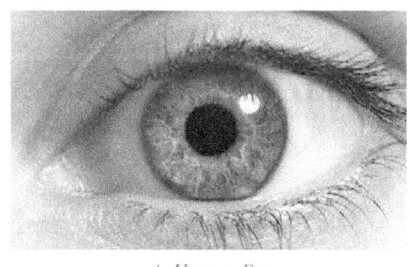

A Human Eye

The peculiar thing about owls is the fact that while they *see clearer at night*, they have an *extraordinary sense of hearing during the day*. It is a matter of great curiosity to all as to how owls can see clearer at night than in the day.

Before we get to that, it is important to know how human beings see things. The light scattered by an object is focussed at our retina by the lenses inside the eyes. An inverted image is formed here which the optic nerves carry to the brain. The brain then inverts the image and we are hence able to see things.

The eyes of an owl are large and forward-pointed. There are four main reasons due to which owls are nocturnal.

Firstly, in the case of an owl, the distance between the retina and lens of the eye is more than that in human beings. This forms bigger images on the retina of the owl.

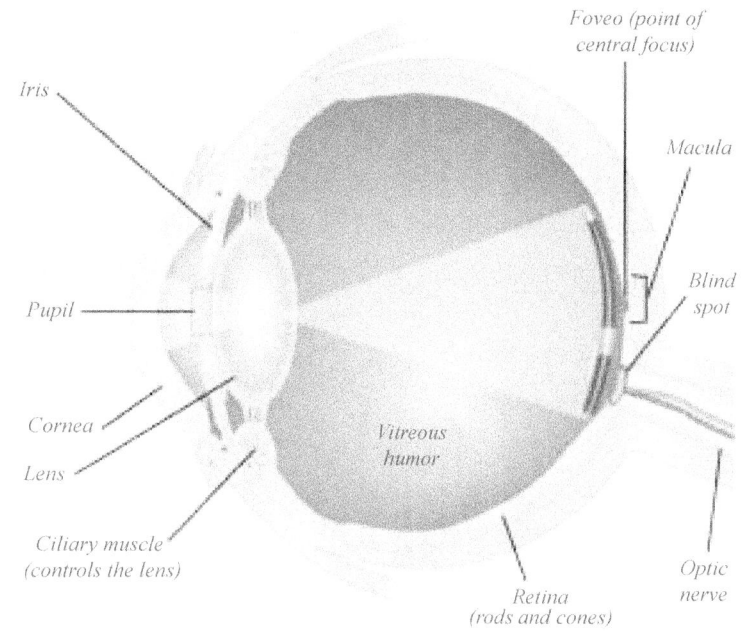

An Owl's Eye

Secondly, an owl's retina has *10,000 rods and cones* per square millimetre compared to the 2,000 in humans. This enables an owl to see five times more than us!

The third reason is a special red-coloured protein, present in an owl's eyes, which makes its vision extremely sensitive to light. Thus, an owl is able to see things clearly, which others may find hazy.

The fourth and final reason for the nocturnal nature of an owl is the fact that the pupil of the eye of an owl can dilate more, resulting in detecting the smallest amount of light.

Because of these four factors, an owl is more comfortable watching things in the night. Due to these properties of its eyes, in daylight, objects appear extremely bright.

Another surprising thing about an owl is that it can rotate its head at an angle of 180 degrees, which is till the back of his head!

- There are around 200 different owl species.
- Owls are active at night (nocturnal).
- A group of owls is called a parliament.
- Most owls hunt insects, small mammals and other birds.
- Some owl species hunt fish.
- Owls have powerful talons (claws) which help them catch and kill prey.
- Owls have large eyes and a flat face.
- Owls can turn their heads as much as 270 degrees.
- Owls are farsighted, meaning they can't see things close to their eyes clearly.
- Owls are very quiet in flight compared to other birds of prey.
- The colour of owl's feathers helps them blend into their environment (camouflage), which also helps them to catch their prey.
- Barn owls can be recognised by their heart shaped face.

Chapter - 7

THE MAP OF MIGRATORY BIRDS

Every year, in the months of spring, millions of birds migrate from colder to temperate regions of the world in order to breed. Basically, they migrate to different places to have abundance of food for them to rear their chicks.

Migratory Birds

Birds need to adjust their metabolic systems to meet the needs of the migration process. Energy storage through fat accumulation and sleep control in nocturnal migrants require special physiological adaptations. Moreover, the feathers of a bird also suffer from wear and tear and need to be moulted. Apart from this, migration also requires changes in the behavioural patterns, such as flying in flocks to reduce the energy used or risk of predation during migration.

The northern parts of North America, Europe, and Asia receive the maximum number of migrations. The southern hemisphere also gets migratory birds, like the double banded dotted flies from Australia to New Zealand to breed. Wild Geese fly north in the northern hemisphere during spring and in autumn, they fly south to breed,

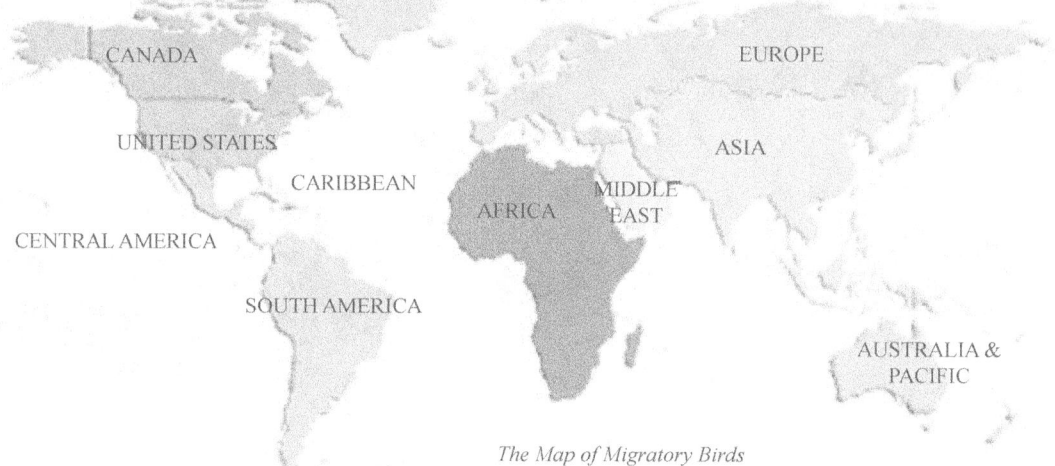

The Map of Migratory Birds

while the American Gold Plover flies about 3325 kilometers non-stop from Alaska to Hawaii.

The main cause behind migration is the change in the length of the day due to changing seasons which ultimately change the birds' hormonal balance.

One may often wonder how exactly a bird is able to find its way from its home region to the migratory place and back. Well, the answer to this query is the proof of a bird's intelligence.

Bats

Like in any other structure where the young ones learn and follow from the old and experienced, even birds follow this principle of migration.

Young birds that are migrating for the first time fly with the older ones who have taken the trip before and guide them through the migration route.

While flying, birds make note of landmarks, such as lakes, mountains, coastlines, etc., to remember their route of migration. Some birds are even intelligent enough to use the sun and stars to navigate to and fro from the migrating region.

Eels

Birds are not the only species that migrate. Many other animals such as mammals, flying insects, fish, locusts, eels, etc., also migrate in order to survive bad weather, breeding problems, etc.

Quick Facts

- The word, 'migration' comes from the Latin word, migratus that means 'to change' and refers to how birds change their geographic locations seasonally.

- Migration peaks in spring and fall, but in reality, there are birds migrating 365 days a year. The actual dates of when birds migrate depends on many factors, including bird species, migration distance, travel speed, route, climate and more.

- Before migrating, many birds enter a state of hyperphagia, where hormone levels compel them to drastically increase their body weight to store fat to use as energy while travelling. Some bird species may as much as double their body weight in the weeks leading up to migration.

- Birds may fly from 15-600 miles or more per day during migration, depending on when they are migrating, how far they have to go and the conditions they face along the route, including the availability of suitable stopovers.

- Hawks, swifts, swallows and waterfowl migrate primarily during the day, while many songbirds migrate at night, in parts to avoid the attention of migrating predators, such as the raptors. The cooler, calmer air at night also makes migration more efficient for many species, while those that migrate during the day most often take advantage of the solar-heated thermal currents for easy soaring.

- Migrating birds use the stars for navigation, as well as the sun, wind patterns and landforms, all of which help guide them to the same locations, each year. The earth's magnetic field also plays a part in how birds migrate.

Chapter - 8

THE COLOUR OF FIREWORKS

Fireworks, often known as fire crackers, are used to celebrate various occasions of happiness, such as weddings, festivals, etc. Once lighted, they explode and burst into a variety of colours, because of which they remain a special attraction amongst children. Over 300 varieties of fireworks are available in today's markets and it is approximated that a sum of Rupees 5,000 crore is spent on the purchase of crackers, each year.

The Colour of Fireworks

People enjoy bursting crackers and looking at the colourful explosions. However, have you ever wondered where the colours in the fireworks come from? Similar to the answers of many general questions that we ponder over, the answer to this one also lies in the world of science.

Fireworks are made from a mixture of potassium nitrate, sulphur, coal, and certain other metal salts. In addition to these, chemicals like strontium, barium, magnesium and sodium are used that add colour to the fireworks. These are combined with potassium chlorate.

The green colour in the fireworks is due to the presence of barium salts, while the production of light blue colour is because of strontium sulphate. The yellow colour is produced by strontium carbonate, whereas strontium nitrate gives red colour. Apart from these, salts of sodium impart shades of yellow, while

Fireworks during Diwali

those of copper are responsible for the production of yellow hues. The silvery rain from the fireworks comes from the presence of aluminium powder.

At the time of explosion, the salts present in the fireworks burn to produce various colours, creating a beautiful and colourful view.

Fireworks were first manufactured in China, thousands of years ago. The trend was shortly followed by various regions of Europe, Arabia, and Greece. In today's date, the largest firework manufacturer of the world is a small town named Sivaski, located in the south of India.

However, we must realise that the bursting of crackers causes harm to the environment. Fireworks cause great amount of pollution which often mixes up with fog in the winter season and creates smog, which is harmful for plants. Moreover, a large number of trees are destroyed, while the production of crackers. Hence, we should burn fireworks as less as possible.

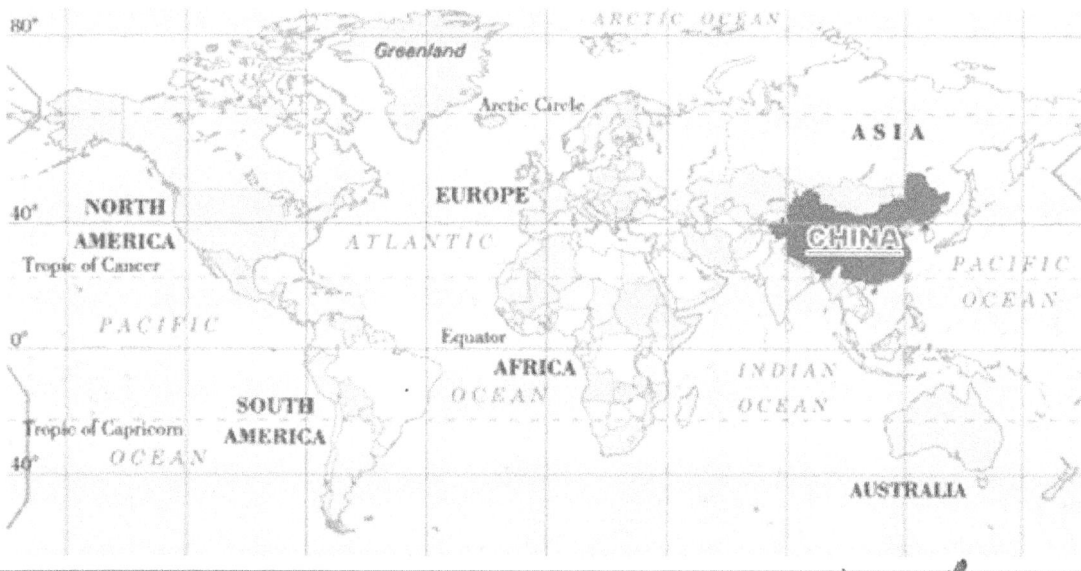

- Creating firework colours is a complex endeavour, requiring considerable art and application of physical science. Excluding propellants or special effects, the points of light ejected from fireworks, termed 'stars', generally require an oxygen-producer, fuel, binder (to keep everything where it needs to be), and colour producer. There are two main mechanisms of colour production in fireworks, *incandescence and luminescence.*

- Incandescence is light produced from heat. Heat causes a substance to become hot and glow, initially emitting infrared, then red, orange, yellow, and white light as it becomes increasingly hotter. When the temperature of a firework is controlled, the glow of components, such as charcoal, can be manipulated to be the desired colour (temperature) at the proper time. Metals, such as aluminum, magnesium and titanium, burn very brightly and are useful for increasing the temperature of the fireworks.

- Luminescence is light produced using energy sources other than heat. To produce luminescence, energy is absorbed by an electron of an atom or molecule, causing it to become excited, but unstable. When the electron returns to a lower energy state the energy is released in the form of a photon (light). The energy of the photon determines its wavelength or colour.

- Sometimes the salts needed to produce the desired

colour are unstable. Barium chloride (green) is unstable at room temperatures, so barium must be combined with a more stable compound (e.g., chlorinated rubber).

- Copper chloride (blue), which is present in fireworks, on the other hand, is unstable at high temperatures, so the firework cannot get too hot, yet must be bright enough to be seen.

Chapter - 9

THE FORMATION OF A RAINBOW

Rainbows are a beautiful play of colours by nature. Appearing after rains, rainbows spread a breeze of cheer and happiness into the hearts of its viewers. A rainbow appears when the sun shines through the rain.

Though sunlight appears white, it consists of seven different shades, namely, *violet, indigo, blue, green, yellow, orange, and red,* abbreviated as VIBGYOR. When sunlight splits into seven colours, the process is called *dispersion*, while the strip of the seven colours is referred to as a **spectrum**.

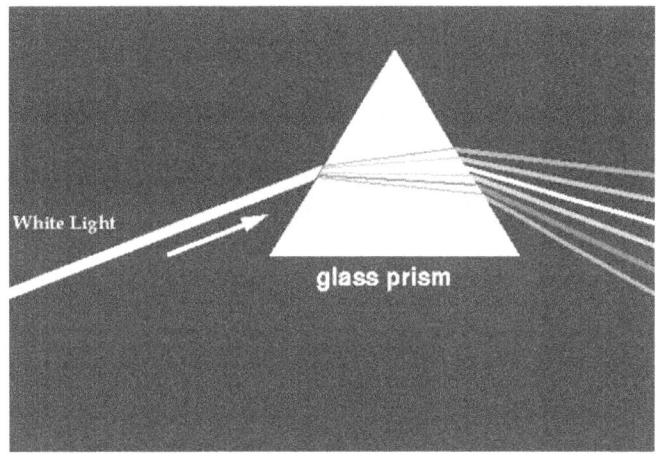

The Spectrum of Light

A rainbow usually appears after rain when tiny drops of water fill the atmosphere. When sunrays fall on these spherical water droplets, they act like prisms. This results in the rays getting refracted and split up into the **VIBGYOR** colours as they pass through the raindrops.

Since each ray of light gets refracted in a different angle from the prism, they separate into seven different colours, forming a **Rainbow**. It also thus proves that white light is made up of seven colours.

The shape of a rainbow is that of a semi-circular arc. This is because the sun is circular. A rainbow is called complete when it has both a primary and a secondary arc. The primary arc has violet on the inner side, followed by indigo, blue, green, yellow, orange and red. In the secondary arc, the order of the colours is reversed. Red colour is on the inner side, while violet is on the outermost.

In a complete rainbow, the location of the secondary arc is above the primary arc. This kind of a rainbow is formed when the sun's rays are reflected and refracted after the first reflection and refraction within the same raindrop.

A rainbow always appears in the opposite direction from the sun. A necessary requirement for the formation of a rainbow is that the sun should shine just after the rain. It is also extremely important for our eyes that the sun and the rainbow lie in the same plane.

Most often, rainbows are formed and seen in the early mornings or late evenings after a heavy shower. A beautiful and vibrant sight, rainbows are a delight to the eyes.

Quick Facts

- A rainbow can be defined as a band of colours (from red on the inside to violet on the outside) assembled as an arc that is formed by reflection and refraction (or bending) of the sun's rays inside raindrops. They appear when it is raining in one part of the sky and sunny in another.

- Most people think the only colours of a rainbow are red, orange, yellow, green, blue, indigo and violet, popularly abbreviated as VIBGYOR but a rainbow is actually made up of an entire continuum of colours—even colours the eye can't see!

- We are able to see the colours of a rainbow because the light of different colours is refracted when it travels from one medium, such as air, into another- in this case, the water of the raindrops. When all the colours that make up sunlight are combined, they look white, but once they are refracted, the colours break up into the ones we see in a rainbow.

Chapter - 10

WHAT IS MILK MADE UP OF?

One often wonders why mothers keep asking their children to have milk every day. While some children love milk, there is an adequate percentage that wonders what exactly the glass of milk contains that prevents it from being substituted by their favourite aerated drink. Well, given below are the many reasons for the same.

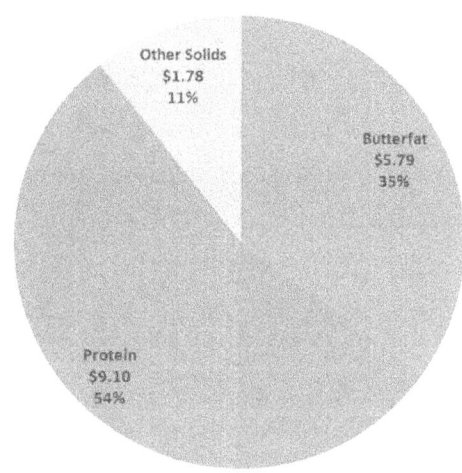

Essential Components in Milk

Milk is a highly nutritious, i.e., the white liquid produced by mammals to feed their young ones. Usually milk obtained from cows and buffaloes is used by human beings. However, in many other parts of the world, milk is obtained from other animals as well. For example, people in northern Europe consume reindeers' milk and those in the Middle East countries consume goats' milk.

A Man Milking a Goat

Milk is often known as the "complete food". This is so because it has all the vital nutrients to ensure our good health. Cow's milk constitutes 87.2% water, 3.5% proteins, 3.7% fat, and 4.9% sugar among other vitamins and minerals. Similarly, different animals have these nutrients too, but in different proportions.

Different nutrients have different qualities. While proteins present in the milk help us to grow and enhance our physical strength, sugar acts as a fuel, and fats give us extra energy. Milk also contains minerals like calcium and phosphorus which help in bone formation. Besides that, vitamins **A, B, C, D, E, K,** and niacin present in milk help reduce vitamin deficiency for healthier growth.

Man started consuming milk over 5,000 years ago and this was the time when he discovered its various uses. Apart from its pure form, many other products of milk, such as *curd, butter, cheese,* etc. can be obtained from milk. Over time, these products have come to use in our domestic lives immensely.

Milk gets spoiled very soon. To prevent its spoilage, it is essential to cool it to 10 degrees celsius within 2 hours from    milking and should be maintained at that temperature at the time of transportation from the source to the destination.

It is advisable to boil milk once before consuming it. This is called pasteurisation. It is done in order to control and stop the growth of micro bacteria in the milk. However, boiling it several times in a day kills its nutrients.

In recent times, many people have begun preferring processed milk due to health reasons. The consumption of homogenised and skimmed milk is ever rising because, through these processes, the fat in the milk is reduced or completely removed.

- Milk is a white liquid produced by the mammary glands of mammals. It is the primary source of nutrition for young mammals before they are able to digest other types of food. Early-lactation milk contains colostrum, which carries the mother's antibodies to the baby and can reduce the risk of many diseases in the baby. It also contains many other nutrients.

- It is basically an emulsion of butterfat globules within a water-based fluid that contains dissolved carbohydrates and protein aggregates with minerals.

- As an agricultural product, milk is extracted from mammals and used as food for humans. In the year, 2011, worldwide dairy farms produced about 730 million tonnes of milk.

- India is the world's largest producer and consumer of milk, yet it neither exports nor imports milk. New Zealand, the European Union's 27 member states, Australia, and the United States are the world's largest exporters of milk and milk products. China and Russia are the world's largest importers of milk and milk products.

Chapter - 11

TELESCOPES

An optical instrument, called a telescope is a tube-like tool used to see distant objects with magnified clarity.

It was invented in 1608 by Hans Lippershey, a Dutch optician. The following year, Galileo made his first telescope with a magnification of thirty. This made him observe the rings of Saturn and the moons of Jupiter.

Hans Lippershey

Galileo Galilei

Today, mainly three kinds of telescopes exist:

  (i) Refracting telescopes

 (ii) Reflecting telescopes

(iii) Radio telescopes

People also use binoculars to observe which are basically two telescopes joine peaks, horse races, etc.

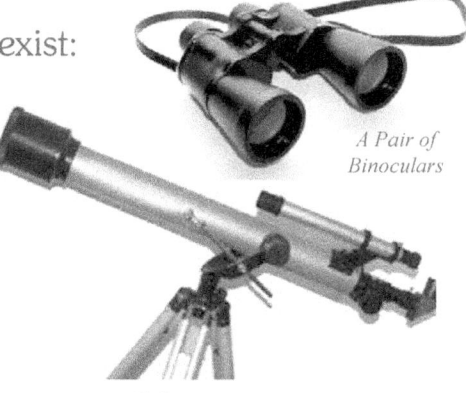
A Pair of Binoculars

Refracting

A **Refracting Telescope** uses its lenses to bend or refract light. It makes use of two lenses fitted together. A larger sized convex objective lens and a convex eye piece is used in an astronomical telescope. However, a **Galilean Telescope** uses a convex lens and a concave eye piece.

Modern day Refracting Telescopes are much more advanced.

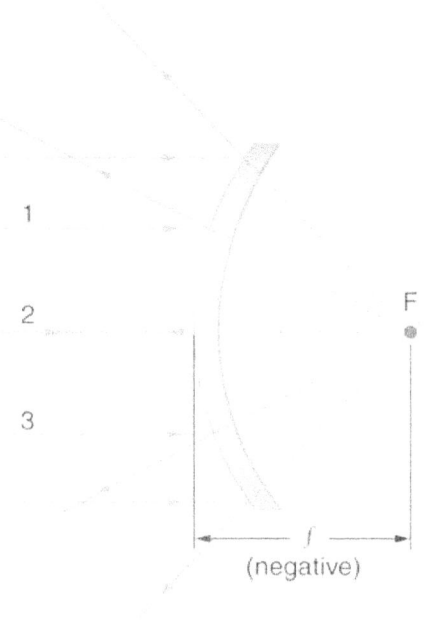

A Convex Mirror with Light Reflecting from it

This kind of a telescope is made of a concave mirror that gathers and focusses light rays. It also has a mirror near the point, where the light rays come together. It reflects back the rays into the eye piece.

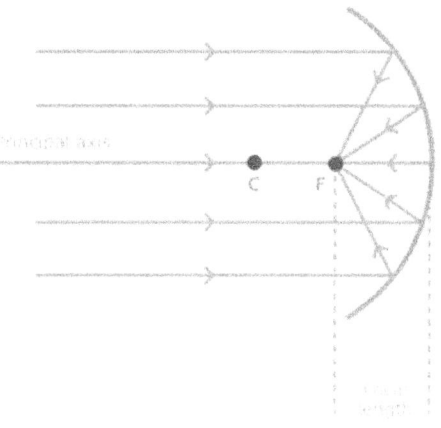

A Concave Mirror with Light Reflecting from it

Radio Telescope

The **Newtonian Telescope** uses a mirror set at an angle of 45 degrees to reflect light into the eye piece.

A **Schmidt - Cassegrain Telescope** has a convex lens. It reflects light into a tiny hole in the centre of the objective mirror.

Radio Telescopes were invented in 1930s. Usually, they contain a dish-shaped radio wave collector. They can see through the clouds and can be used at any time of the day as their work is based on radio waves rather than light.

The largest radio dish collector in the world is of 305 metres in diameter.

Reflecting Telescope

Quick Facts

- Dutchman Hans Lippershey invented the telescope in 1608, but legend has it that the device was really invented three years earlier by kids playing with lenses in a spectacle-maker's shop.

- Telescopes gave rise to the first high-speed telecommunication networks: spyglasses that were used to relay semaphore signals from miles away.

- Galileo was the first to turn the telescope skyward, leading to the discovery of Jupiter's satellites and craters on the moon. Less cleverly, he also pointed his telescope at the sun, which may have triggered his later blindness.

- Ireland's "Leviathan of Parsonstown," a 40-ton reflecting telescope built by the Earl of Rosse in 1845, was the world's largest for seven decades. But wet weather kept it shut down most of the time.

- To deliver the 100-inch mirror for the Hooker Telescope on Mount Wilson in California, nearly 200 men with ropes guided a truck along a tortuous, eight-hour drive to the top but it was worth it. The Hooker Telescope proved that other galaxies exist and that the universe is expanding.

- Today, using an Internet-based Telescope such as the Seeing in the Dark scope at New Mexico Skies, any amateur can command a robotic observatory while lounging at home. Most professional astronomers now work that way too, operating telescopes remotely with computers and rarely looking through an eyepiece.

- The NASA or the National Aeronautics and Space Administration is the agency of the United States government that is responsible for the nation's civilian space program and for aeronautics and aerospace research. Since February 2006, the NASA's mission statement has been to "pioneer the future in space exploration, scientific discovery and aeronautics research." The NASA launched the Hubble Space Telescope in 1990, seven years later with a budget of over $ 2 million.

Chapter - 12

WHY ARE SOME STARS BIGGER THAN THE OTHERS?

While gazing at the night sky, one can easily observe that some stars appear bigger than the others. While looking at the stars through a telescope, one can spot the differences in the brightness and colour of the various stars.

Stars in the Night Sky

Have you ever wondered why this is so? The features of a star are very mysterious. They are never constant and change depending upon many factors.

The temperature of a star determines its colour and brightness. If the temperature of the star is high, its brightness increases. In other words, there is a direct relationship between the temperature of a star and its brightness.

The brightness of a star depends on the relationship between its colour and temperature. Together, these two factors determine if the star would shine bright or not. Stars that appear red or yellow have the lowest surface temperature. Stars that are yellow or green have a slightly higher temperature. These are followed by white-coloured stars. *Stars that appear blue have the highest surface temperature.*

The temperature of the stars that are blue in colour can be as high as 27,750 degrees celsius. The Sun is a yellow star. Knowing this, we can just imagine how much hotter a blue star can be.

The typical temperature of a yellow star is about 6,000 degrees celsius. Stars that appear red or fainter yellow are

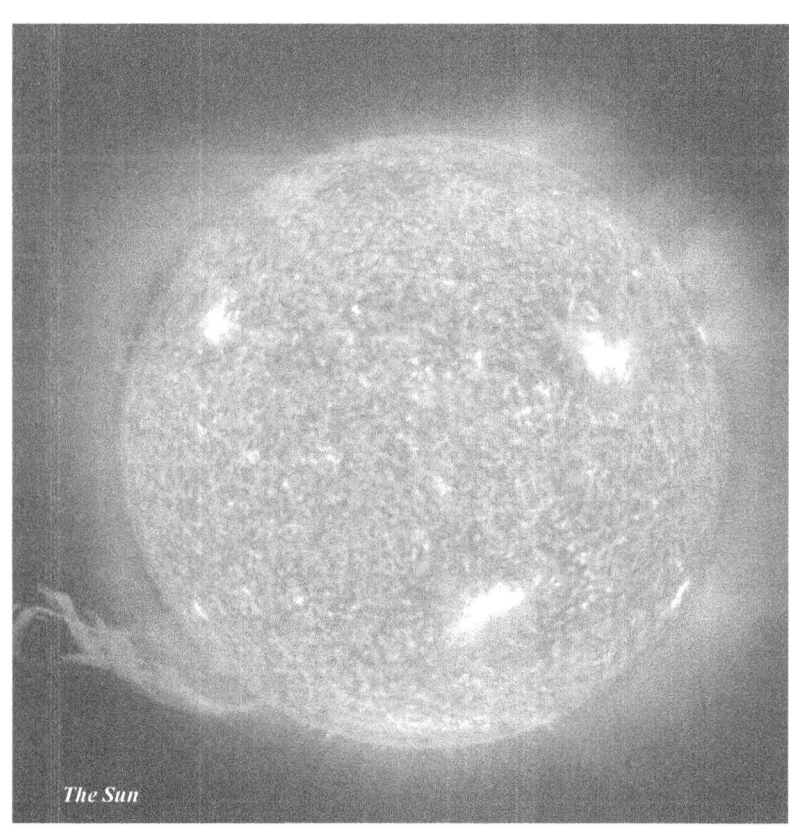

The Sun

comparatively cooler, with an approximate temperature of 1,650 degrees celsius. The above mentioned facts imply that the brightness of stars is directly related to their surface temperature.

Apart from this, another factor that determines the brightness of a star is its distance from us. If the star is farther away, it appears *fainter*, whereas a star close to our planet shines *bright*.

It can also happen that stars that are much brighter than others due to their surface temperature may not shine distinctly in the night sky because their distance from our planet is enormous.

This situation is comparable to that of street lamps. The lamps that are closer to our vision appear brighter than the ones that are away from us.

Quick Facts

- Stars are all made up of matter...so this question could be addressed as; how do forming stars obtain more matter?. The answer is simply more gravity. Gravity is defined as the force of attraction between two masses. So as the star attracts more matter, its gravity increases and this process of attracting matter speeds up.

- But the only way gravity can increase is if there is plenty of matter available. Matter isn't spread out uniformly across the universe and often, it's clustered in vast 'pockets' of gases and particles called 'Nebulae'.

- These are where stars are born. If a star is forming inside a particular large Nebula, it has more matter available, and therefore, the stars' gravity can continue to grow and create a larger star than a star in a Nebula with less matter.

However, the above reason is certainly not the only reason how a star size varies, but is the easiest to explain. It's also easier to understand as our Sun was created inside the same Nebula as other local stars which is why we don't find particularly larger stars close to the Earth; which is probably a good thing.

Chapter - 13

WHO MEASURED THE UNIVERSE?

One may often wonder if it is possible for the universe to be measured. The universe consists of not only the Earth and the Solar System, but also stars, galaxies etc. Considering these facts, it may seem impossible to have an 3exact measurement of the universe.

The universe is beyond imagination. It is impossible for a layman to think about estimating the measure of the universe. Over time,

The Universe

many scientists and astronomers have attempted to solve this huge task but it continued to stay a riddle for a long time.

This scientific breakthrough was made by American astronomer, **Edwin Hubble**. He was the first scientist to successfully measure distances beyond our galaxy, the *Milky Way* or the *'Akash Ganga'* as it is called in the Indian Astronomy.

Edwin Hubble came up with various theories. One of them was the **Hubble's Law** which states that the distant galaxies are receding from each other at greater speed than the galaxies closer to ours.

Edwin Powell Hubble

He used the largest telescope available (2.5 metres, on Mount Wilson, California) and tried measuring the universe. He succeeded in measuring the distance of stars in the **Andromeda Galaxy**. He did so by measuring the brightness of the stars. Through this, he could judge how far the stars were from each other. Due to doubts about the brightness of the stars, he obtained a result of about 8,00,000 light years. At present, it is about two million light years away.

If we go by the Hubble's Law, the speed of the galaxies is proportional to the distance between them. This represents the modern day picture of Cosmology. It suggests that all galaxies were once very close to each other and it was only in time that they receded from each other. This concept even supports the **Big Bang Theory** which talks about similar things.

Walter Baade

The actual measurement of the universe did not come forth till a long time. It was only around the time of World War II that the renowned astronomer, **Walter Buade** was able to determine the actual measurement of

galactic distances. His observations proved Edwin Hubble wrong. It came out that the universe was much larger than what Hubble had estimated.

Quick Facts

- **The top ranked scientific justification for building the Hubble Telescope was to determine the size and age of the Universe through observations of Cepheid variables in distant galaxies. This scientific goal was so important that it put constraints on the lower limit of the size of Hubble's primary mirror.**

- **Cepheids are a special type of variable stars with very stable and predictable brightness variations. The period of these variations depends on the physical properties of the stars, such as their mass and true brightness. This means that astronomers, just by looking at the variability of their light, can find out about the Cepheids' physical nature, which then can be used very effectively to determine their distances. For this reason, cosmologists call Cepheids as 'standard candles'.**

- **Astronomers have used the Hubble Telescopes to observe Cepheids with extraordinary results. The Cepheids have then been used as stepping-stones to make distance measurements for supernovae, which have, in turn, given a measure for the scale of the Universe. Today, we know the age of the Universe to a much higher precision than before.**

Chapter - 14

HOW ARE DATES DETERMINED?

Over time, man has realised that stars are not mere objects to look at and admire. There are innumerable stars in the sky and since times immemorial; they have helped man in various ways.

The pole star is known as a guiding star as it leads man to his bearings. Concepts like astronomy have emerged from the study of these tiny sparkles in the sky. Man has always been fascinated with stars and has hence invented powerful telescopes to study them. In time, he has been able to extract valuable information about them.

One of the many wonderful things about stars is that one can determine dates with their help. In order to understand how, we have to undertake an activity.

In order to determine the date, make a circle of at least 8 inches diameter on a large sheet of paper. Then, divide the circle into 12 equal parts, in the same way a clock face is divided.

The Pole Star

Now, write the name of each month on each division of the paper. At the position of 12 o' clock, write the month, March and following the usual order of months, list them anti-clockwise.

Locate the centre of the circle and mark it as the 'North Star'. Now, imagine the distance between every month on the circle which is further divided into 30 parts.

Next, take the sheet of paper out on a clear night and hold it in such a way that March is on the top. Visualise the diagram in the night sky with the **North Star** in the centre. Take note of the location of the **Bid Dipper** and draw it on the diagram in the same way you find it in the sky. After this, draw a straight line from the pointer to the North Star. The line drawn will pass through the circle at a point which will indicate the date of when the observation has been taken.

For example, if the line passes between June and July, it is the 15th of June. It is important to draw a large circle, or else, it would be difficult to find the exact date. One can only come near the actual date.

The vital part is to remember that on the diagram, if an observation is made at midnight on a particular date, the pointers should be in the line with that date on the star calendar. This is the way of finding the date with the help of stars.

The Big Dipper

- The Gregorian Calendar is today's internationally accepted civil calendar and is also known as the 'Western Calendar' or the 'Christian Calendar'. It was named after the man who first introduced it in February 1582 called Pope Gregory XIII.

- The calendar is strictly a *solar calendar* based on a 365-day common year divided into 12 months of irregular lengths. Each month consists of either 30 or 31 days with 1 month consisting of 28 days during the common year. A Leap Year usually occurs after every 4 years which adds an extra day to make the second month of February, 29 days long rather than 28 days.

- The *Gregorian Calendar* reformed the *Julian Calendar* because the Julian Calendar introduced an error of 1 day, every 128 years. However, a number of days had to be dropped when the change was made.

- The Gregorian Calendar was first adopted in Italy, Poland, Portugal and Spain in 1582.

- The rule for calculating Leap Years was changed to include that a year is a Leap Year if:

  a) The year is evenly divisible by 4.

  b) If the year can be evenly divided by 100, it is NOT a leap year, unless the year is also evenly divisible by 400. Then it is a leap year.

Chapter - 15

WHY DON'T WE FEEL THE EARTH'S MOTION?

Earlier, it was believed that the Earth was the centre of the universe and all objects, the Sun, the Moon, and other Planets revolved around it. This assumption was based on the fact that the Earth was stationary while the placement of the stars and planets seemed to change over time.

The Planet, Earth

The breakthrough to this false belief came when **Nicholas Copernicus**, a Polish astronomer, who put forth his theory of the Earth's revolution around the Sun.

It was hence proved that the Earth revolves around the Sun and completes one full revolution in *365 and one-fourth days*. This is the *period of one year according to the calendar*.

Also, it was proved that the Earth rotates along its own axis which makes a *vertical angle of 23 and half degrees*. One rotation gets completed in *24 days and this makes one full day*.

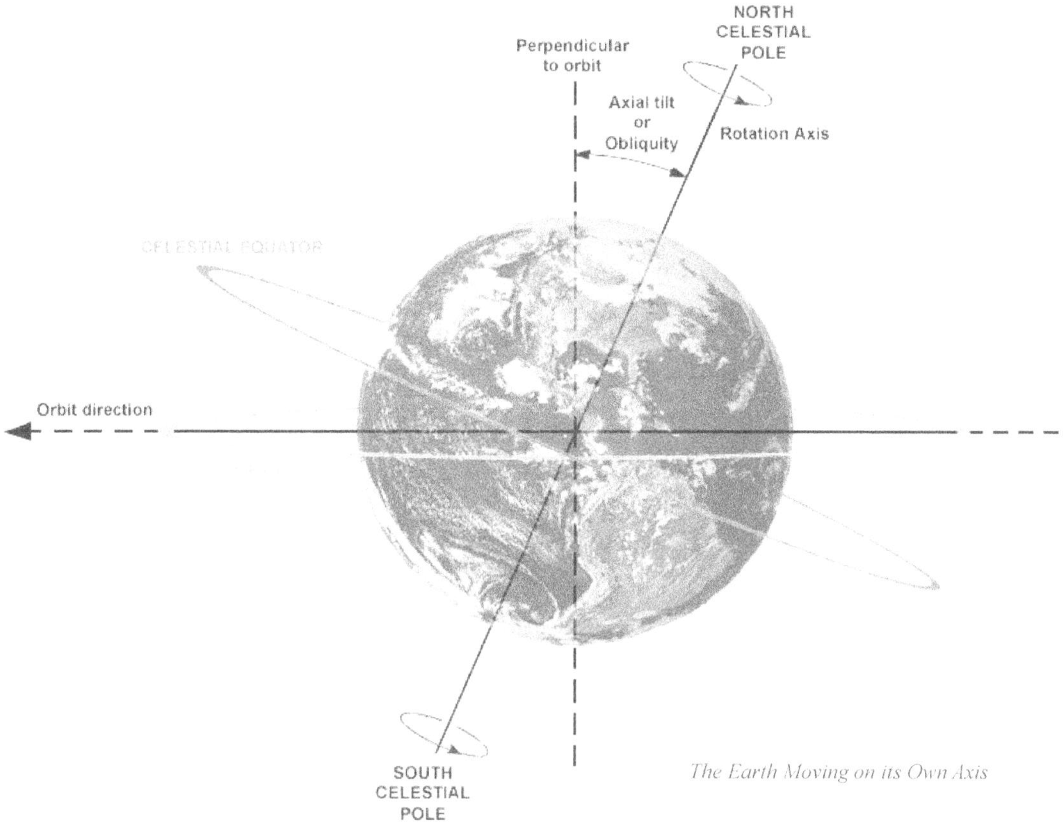

Perpendicular to orbit

NORTH CELESTIAL POLE

Axial tilt or Obliquity

Rotation Axis

CELESTIAL EQUATOR

Orbit direction

SOUTH CELESTIAL POLE

The Earth Moving on its Own Axis

The question that arises is, if the *Earth rotates and revolves at the same* time, why do'nt we feel any motion? It is because of the force of gravity. All things on this Earth move along with it and hence, we don't feel it.

It is like an ant on a rotating football. The ant doesn't feel any movement because it moves with the ball. Similarly, all objects on the Earth move along with it. Hence, we are unable to feel any kind of motion of the Earth as it rotates or revolves.

The *change of seasons* is the biggest proof of the Earth's motion. The seasons change because of the *Earth's revolution* around the Sun and also because of its *rotation along its own axis*. Day and night are also caused because of rotation as the part of the Earth that faces the Sun, *experiences day* while the *other experiences night*.

If the Earth did not rotate, the part facing the Sun would always get day, while the other would experience night all the time. The Earth's, axis makes a vertical angle of 23 and half degrees. As a result of this, the North Pole and the South Pole faces the Sun for six continuous months. This explains the six-month duration of days and nights at the poles.

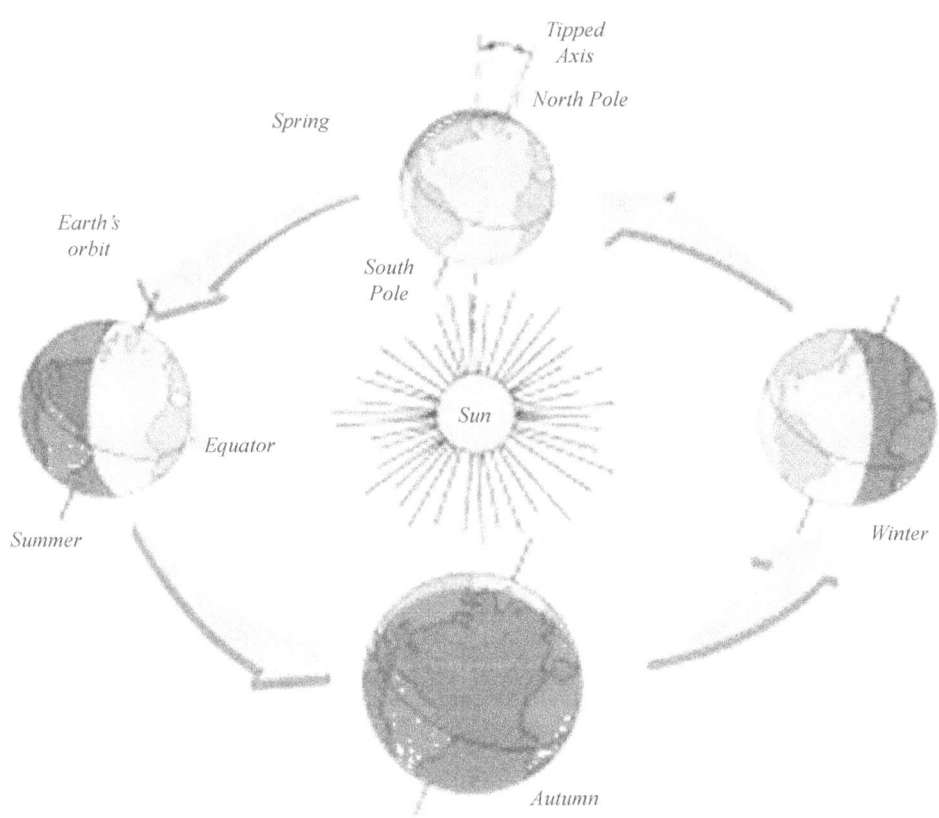

Sunlight Hitting Different Parts of the Earth

The day and night are caused by the Earth's rotation, while the change of seasons occurs due to its revolution around the Sun.

- We don't feel the Earth spin because along with us, the atmosphere, skyscrapers, and everything else are spinning along at the same constant speed.

- It's the same sensation as when you're riding in a car or flying in a plane – as long as the ride is going smoothly. A jumbo jet flies at about 500 miles per hour – that's about 800 kilometers an hour – about half as fast as the Earth spins at its Equator. But if you close your eyes, you don't feel like you're moving at all. And when the flight attendant comes by and pours coffee into your cup, the coffee doesn't fly to the back of the aeroplane. That's because the coffee, the cup and you are all moving at the same speed as the plane.

- Likewise, the Earth is moving at a fixed rate – and we're all moving along with it. Now imagine being on the jumbo jet again – think about what happens when the pilot suddenly speeds up or slows down the plane. You sometimes sense this change as a feeling of being pushed into your seat. In the same way, if the Earth were suddenly to speed up or slow down, you would definitely feel it.

- But as long as the Earth spins steadily – and moves at a constant rate in orbit around the Sun – you as an Earthly passenger move right along with it.

- If the Earth suddenly started to speed up, we'd fall over backwards, and we'd have to lean into the direction of the motion to stand.

Chapter - 16

HOW FAR IS A STAR?

The innumerable stars that brighten a night sky are made up of hot gases. Even the Sun is a star. However, there are various other stars that are brighter than the Sun but cannot be seen by us. This is because of their distance from the Earth. Stars may look like tiny dots in the sky but are actually really big, some even bigger than planets. They appear small to us because they are very far away. Have you ever thought exactly how far stars are from the Earth?

The unit of measuring distance of stars is light years. One light year is referred to the distance travelled by light in one year, the velocity of light being three hundred thousand kilometers per second. The star nearest to the Earth is the Sun. It is followed by a star called the Proxima Centauri, whose distance from the Earth is about 4.28 light years. However, this star is only visible in the southern hemisphere.

The nearest star which is visible from the northern hemisphere is Sirius, also called the Dog Star. From the Earth, it is around 8.8 light years away. Apart from these, another important neighboring star is the Alpha Centauri, which is 4.37 light years away from our planet.

The star farthest from us which is visible to our naked eye is more than 8 million light years away from Earth. If a powerful telescope is used, one can see stars that are a 1,000 times more distant.

It may sound shocking but it is true that there are some stars in this universe that are so far away from us that their light takes more than a 1,000 million years to reach us.

Stars contain the greatest secrets about the universe. Studying the evolution of a star can help reveal many unknown facts about our galaxy and planet. It is due to this reason that since times immemorial, people have been curious about the tiny sparkles we enjoy gazing at in the night.

A Boy Looking at the Stars with a Telescope

From way back in time, people have been inventing newer devices to expose the secrets of stars. Over time, scientists have created a variety of *optical and radio telescopes* for the study of stars. They have been successful in gaining knowledge about these heavenly bodies, but there is still a lot which is yet to be discovered.

- Stars are cosmic energy engines that produce heat, light, ultraviolet rays, x-rays, and other forms of radiations. They are composed largely of gases and plasma, a superheated state of matter composed of subatomic particles.

- Though the most familiar star, our own Sun, stands alone, about three of every four stars exist as part of a binary system containing two mutually orbiting stars.

- No one knows how many stars exist, but the number would be staggering. Our universe likely contains more than 100 billion galaxies, and each of these galaxies may have more than 100 billion stars.

- Some stars have always stood out from the rest. Their brightness is a factor of how much energy they put out, which is called their luminosity, and also how far away from the Earth they are.

- Stars may occur in many sizes, which are classified in a range from dwarfs to supergiants. Supergiants may have radii a thousand times larger than that of our own Sun.

- Hydrogen is the primary building block of stars. The gas circles through space in cosmic dust clouds called the Nebulae. In time, gravity causes these clouds to condense and collapse in on themselves. As they get smaller, the clouds spin faster because of the conservation of angular momentum. Young stars are called Protostars. As they develop, they accumulate mass from the clouds around them and grow into what are known as main sequence stars. The main sequence stars like our own Sun exist in a state of nuclear fusion during which they will emit energy for billions of years by converting hydrogen to helium.

Chapter - 17

THE MASS OF THE EARTH

Whenever a body has to be measured, it is done through the use of a **weighing balance**. The balance is in accordance with the object to be weighed. Our planet, Earth is a giant object. Hence, to weigh the Earth, thinking of a weighing scale is impossible.

An interesting story lies behind the weighing of the Earth.

Newton was a great scientist and made many advancements in the field of science. He introduced theories and laws that are widely used even today. Actually, scientifically, to weigh the Earth, *Newton's law of gravitation is used.*

This law states that there exists a force of attraction between any two bodies in the universe and this is dependent on the masses of the two bodies as well as on the distance between them. Moreover, the force of attraction is directly proportional to the product of the masses of the two bodies and inversely proportional to the square of distances between them.

Weighing the Earth

To determine the mass of the Earth, an experiment is conducted. It is done with the help of the above mentioned law.

In the first step of this experiment, a small metallic ball is suspended with the help of a thin piece of thread. Then, the accurate position of the ball is determined. After this, a huge lead ball that weighs a ton is brought close to the ball. When this

Sir Isaac Newton

is done, the small ball is attracted towards the big lead ball and moves from its initial position. This change in position is due to the gravitational force. In this case, it is less than one-tenth of an inch.

This displacement can be accurately measured. It is done very accurately and carefully with the help of precision instruments.

Through this concept of measuring displacement, the mass of the Earth has been determined. The approximate mass of the Earth is calculated to be somewhere around 5980,000,000,000,000,000,000 tonnes!

Hence, it is only apt to say that to calculate the mass of the Earth is a very tough task and can be done only with the help of Science.

Quick Facts

* **The Earth is the biggest of all the terrestrial planets. A terrestrial planet is a dense planet found in the inner Solar System. The diameter of Earth is 7,926 miles. The circumference measured around the equator is 24,901 miles. There are currently almost 7 billion people living on the Earth. About 30% of the Earth's surface is covered with land, while about 70% is covered by oceans.**

- Our planet, the Earth is an oasis of life in an otherwise desolate universe. The Earth's temperature, weather, atmosphere and many other factors are just right to keep us alive.

- The Earth is about 4.5 billion years old.

- The size of the Earth is approximately 7,926.41 miles (12,756.32 km) in equatorial diameter.

- The surface area of the Earth is around 196,800,000 square miles (509,700,000 square km)

- The atmospheric composition of the Earth is: Nitrogen (78%), Oxygen (1%), Argon (1%), with other gases making up the remainder.

- CRUST COMPOSITION: Oxygen (46.6%), silicon (27.7%), aluminum (8.1%), iron (5%), calcium (3.6%), sodium (2.8%), potassium (2.6%), magnesium (2%), and other elements making up the remainder.

- TEMPERATURE: Ranging from 136 degrees Fahrenheit (58 degrees Celsius) to -128.6 degrees Fahrenheit (-89.6 degrees Celsius). 57 degrees Fahrenheit (14 degrees Celsius) average

- ONE DAY: 23 hours, 56 minutes, 4.09 seconds (We round this to 24 hours.)

- ONE YEAR: 365 days, 6 hours, 9 minutes, 9.54 seconds (We round this upto 365 days)

- NATURAL SATELLITES: 1

- DISTINCTIVE FEATURE: Only planet that supports life.

Chapter - 18

THE TWINKLING OF STARS

One of the first things that a toddler learns is the famous rhyme, 'Twinkle twinkle little star…'

From the young ones to the elderly people, everybody enjoys gazing at the night sky at one time or the other. Their mesmerising sight has the power to appeal to the senses.

Stars radiate light in all directions. Though they appear small, some stars are even bigger than the Earth itself. Have you ever wondered why the stars in the sky twinkle?

The **atmosphere** blankets the Earth, protecting it from

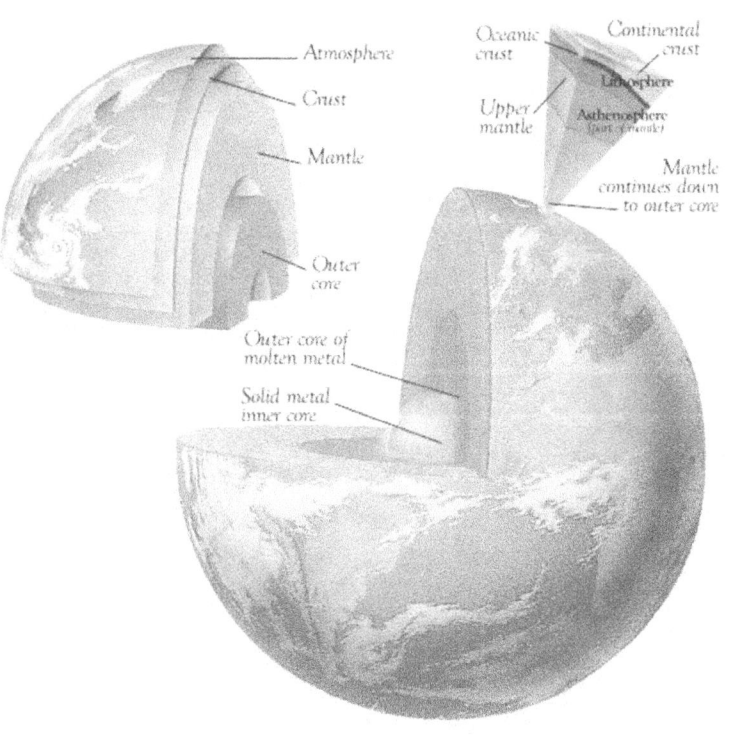

The Sun is also a Star

harmful radiations that come from the outer space. Beyond it is a huge **vacuum**. The atmosphere consists of various gases which are always in motion. Due to their movements, the density of the atmosphere is never constant. Moreover, the refractive index of air varies from place to place.

The light of a star, after entering the Earth's atmosphere, gets deviated a number of times due to the changing densities and consequent changes in the refractive index of the air.

Refraction refers to the degree of change or deviation in the path of light when it enters from one medium to the other. And Iindeed, it is due to refraction that the stars twinkle. Due to the changing refractive index of the air, the light coming from the stars gets refracted at different angles before reaching our eyes. This leads to the fluctuation of light entering into our eyes.

Knowing this, one may wonder why other planets or the moon does not twinkle. This is because while stars are smaller in size, planets are bigger. Stars can be considered as point-like structures in the night sky. However, planets are an extended source or a collection of the point size sources of light. So much so, that they cancel out the effect of twinkling.

Also, due to larger angles, the deviation of the path of light from the moon and planets does not get detected by our eyes. Thus, they don't appear to twinkle.

The Twinkling Stars at Night

- The stars do not twinkle. Their light gets distorted by the churning gases in the Earth's atmosphere. We only notice the twinkling as stars are tiny points of light and are thousands of light-years away, whereas, planets don't twinkle as they're close enough to appear as tiny discs.

- Stars are generally huge balls of gases in outer space. Made from hydrogen, helium and other elements, stars produce light, heat and other forms of energy.

- Stars are in constant conflict with themselves. The collective gravity of all the mass of a star is pulling it inward. If there was nothing to stop it, the star would just continue collapsing for millions of years until it became its smallest possible size; maybe as a neutron star.

- The nuclear fusion at the core of a star generates a tremendous amount of energy. The photons push outward as they make their journey from inside the star to reach the surface; a journey that can take 100,000 years. When stars become more luminous, they expand outward becoming red giants. And when they run out of the light pressure, they collapse down into white dwarfs.

Chapter - 19

THE FORCE OF GRAVITY

It is a known fact that there exists an invisible force on our Earth which pulls all objects towards the centre of the Earth. It is because of this force that everything that is thrown up comes back, and this force is called **gravity**.

Apple Falling due to Gravitational Force

The centre of gravity lies at the centre of the Earth. Hence, if a hole is drilled in the Earth, from one side to the other and an object is thrown inside from one side, it will stop at the centre due to gravity and not come out of the other end.

Also, the weight of a body will be more if it is close to the centre of the Earth. Similarly, the body would weigh less if it is away from it. This is the reason why *things weigh more at the Poles than at the Equator, because the Poles are closer to the centre of the Earth.*

Not only the Earth, but all the planets have this force of gravity. In fact, all objects of the universe attract each other. It is this force which keeps all the objects in their place. This force is also responsible for

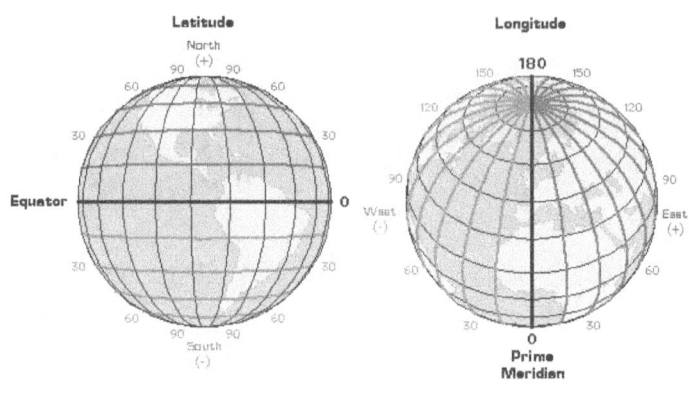

Globe showing Latitudes and Longitudes

the revolution of the Moon around the Earth and the Earth around the Sun.

It is obvious that the *Moon also attracts the Earth*. This is the reason behind the *tides in the seas*.

Till the 16th century, it was believed that in vacuum, if two bodies were dropped from the same height simultaneously, the heavier body would hit the ground first. However, this assumption was broken by **Galileo Galilei**. He proved that irrespective of their masses, all objects dropped from the same point at the same time would hit the ground together in a vacuum.

He did so by throwing two balls of different masses from the Leaning Tower of Pisa in front of a thousand people.

Subsequently, Newton declared the law of gravity which states that, the force of attraction between two bodies is directly proportional to the product of their masses and inversely proportional to the square of the distance between them. Hence, if the mass of one of the two bodies is doubled, the force of attraction between them also doubles.

However, if the distance between the two objects is doubled, the force of attraction between them will reduce by one- fourth of the initial value.

Quick Facts

- On Earth, the acceleration due to gravity is 9.8m/sec^2

- The Universal Gravity Constant is 6.7E-11.

- Sir Isaac Newton came up with the idea of gravity when he saw an apple fall from a tree.

- The force of gravity decreases as you get farther away from the Earth.

- The force of gravity increases with an object of mass.

- Gravity is caused as a result of space and time woven together.

- In a circular orbit, the centrifugal force is equal to the gravitational force.

- The force of gravity on the Moon is smaller than the force of gravity on the Earth.

- The gravitational force is smaller than the electric force when compared with the same mass.

Chapter - 20

ASTRONAUTS

Astronauts, also called *cosmonauts*, are highly trained professionals who travel to space. Explorers of the universe, these astronauts get trained by a human spaceflight program to become members of a spacecraft.

An Astronauts in Space

The first person to ever go into space was **Yuri Gagarin** in **1961**. He orbited around the Earth for 108 minutes. The first woman in space was **Valentina Tereshkova**, who orbited the Earth for almost 3 days. The youngest space traveller was **Gherman Titov**, who was 25 when he flew on a spacecraft. He was also the first to suffer 'space sickness.' On the other hand, the oldest astronaut was **John Glenn**, who flew at the age of 77.

Yuri Gagarin

For the execution of a project, different astronauts have different designations and duties.

- A Pilot Astronaut has the onboard responsibility of the crew, vehicle, success of the mission, and safety of the flight.

- A Mission Specialist Astronaut coordinates all the operations of the shuttle. They are expected to have a detailed knowledge of the shuttle and objectives of the mission as they perform extravehicular activities and assist in experiment operations.

- A Payload Specialist is an additional member to the crew who may be needed for certain specific tasks, depending oupon the need of the operation.

While on a project, astronauts consume specially processed food which is easy to store and eat in the low-gravity environment. It is usually in the form of toothpaste tubes and contains all the vital nutrients that help to maintain the health of the astronauts.

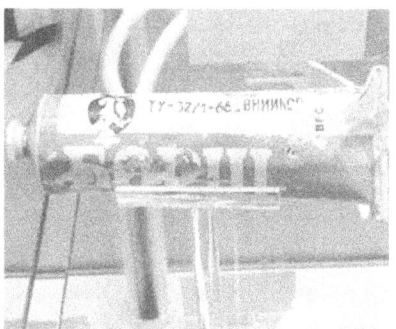
Food for Astronauts

The National Aeronautics and Space Administration (NASA) first selected astronauts for training in 1959. Although the requirements to become an astronaut today are very high, the first selected **John Glenn** and **Scott Carpenter**, of the **Mercury Seven Group**, did not have a college degree at the time of selection.

An Astronaut in Space Suit

In today's times, the NASA has laid down an extremely challenging requirement list for aspiring astronauts. The basic requirements for an astronaut include a bachelor's degree in engineering, biological science, physical science or mathematics, and at least 1,000 hours of pilot-in-command experience in a jet aircraft. Also, they are required to pass a physical test that includes distant visual acuity: 20/100, blood pressure: 140/90 measured in a sitting position and height between 62 and 75 inches.

After selection, the chosen astronauts go through an extensive training of 20 months to become competent of experiencing the conditions of space. This includes training for Extra-vehicular Activities (EVA) in the Neutral Buoyancy Laboratory, periods of weightlessness in the KC-135, also called the 'vomit comet', and flight experience of the T-38 jet aircraft.

Quick Facts

- In space, it is not possible to breathe air normally, so an astronaut's spacesuit is outfitted with oxygen so that he/she can breathe when working outside of the spacecraft.

- Astronauts can urinate while wearing their spacesuits outside the spacecraft. He or she usually wears a maximum absorbency garment (MAG), which can hold up to two litres of fluid.

- Astronauts sleep in bunk beds or in sleeping bags. However, these bunk beds must be fitted with buckles so that the astronauts can buckle up. Otherwise, they might float around the spacecraft while sleeping.

- They can choose from 70 different types of food. However, the food will either be already prepackaged for them or need just a very small amount of preparation. Sometimes, when the astronauts are eating, the food will float around, as there is no gravity.

- While not actively working, astronauts can read books, watch movies, or talk to family and friends on Earth. They can even use an exercise bike. (they have to do a lot of exercise to stay healthy.)

- The first living animal in orbit was a dog from Russia called Laika. It travelled into space on Sputnik 2 in 1957.

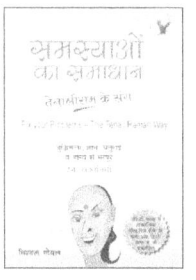

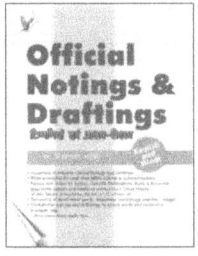

STUDENT DEVELOPMENT/LEARNING
(छात्र विकास/लर्निंग)

JOKES
(हास्य)

MAGIC & FACT (जादू एवं तथ्य)

MUSIC (संगीत)

COMPUTER

Quiz Books
(प्रश्नोत्तरी की पुस्तकें)

MYSTERIES
(रहस्य)

DRAWING BOOKS (ड्राइंग बुक्स)

BIOGRAPHIES (आत्म कथाएँ)

 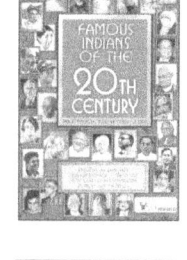

PUZZLES (पहेलियां)

ACTIVITIES BOOK (एक्टिविटीज बुक)

CHILDREN'S ENCYCLOPEDIA
(बच्चों के ज्ञानकोश)

CHILDREN'S ENCYCLOPEDIA
THE WORLD OF KNOWLEDGE

Code: 02152 S

All Books in Full Colour

Free CD for additional reference

Set of 5 Books in Attractive Gift Box

71 SERIES (71 श्रृंखला)

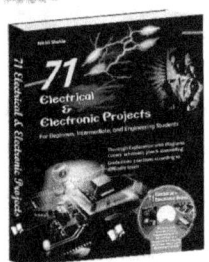

All books available at www.vspublishers.com

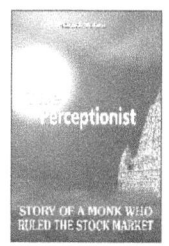

CHILDREN TALES
(बच्चों की कहानियाँ)

TALES & STORIES
(कथा एवं कहानियाँ)

All Books Fully Coloured

Save ₹ 150/-
Pay ₹ 600/- instead of
₹ 750/- for complete
Set of 5 books price
₹ 150/- each

Gift Pack

HINDI LITERATURE
(हिन्दी साहित्य)

www.ingramcontent.com/pod-product-compliance
Lightning Source LLC
Chambersburg PA
CBHW080748250626
47162CB00010B/3067